PETER RABBIT

BATTLE FOR THE GARDEN

F. WARNE & Cº

MEET THE CHARACTERS

Peter

Flopsy

Mopsy

Cotton-tail

Benjamin

Mr. Jeremy
Fisher

Mrs. Tiggy-winkle

Squirrel
Nutkin

Pigling Bland

Jemima Puddle-duck

Tommy Brock

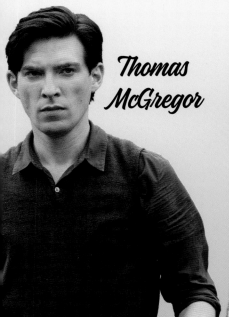

Thomas McGregor

Bea

Old Mr. McGregor

Most vegetable gardens are peaceful places, where crunchy carrots, crisp radishes, and juicy tomatoes grow. But **not** this vegetable garden . . .

This patch of green was a battleground between a gardener named **Mr. McGregor** and a furry little rabbit named **Peter**.

Normally, Peter Rabbit would **sneak** into the garden to find some food. After all, the garden belonged to Peter **and his family** before the McGregors showed up.

Peter usually got away with food for his sisters and cousin.

But Mr. McGregor always chased him out. Luckily, not all humans are bad.

Sometimes **Bea,** their human friend, would need to rescue him.

Every day, Mr. McGregor would spot Peter in his blue coat and shout,

"RABBIT! I'M GOING TO PUT YOU IN A PIE!"

Peter would shout . . . well, nothing, because rabbits don't talk to humans.

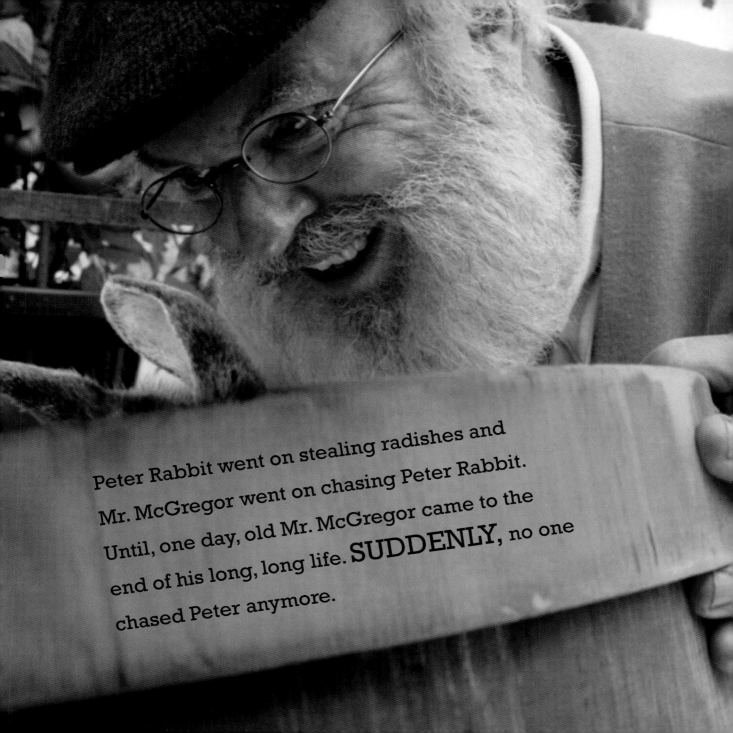

Peter Rabbit went on stealing radishes and Mr. McGregor went on chasing Peter Rabbit. Until, one day, old Mr. McGregor came to the end of his long, long life. SUDDENLY, no one chased Peter anymore.

Now, **everything** belonged to Peter, his sisters, Flopsy, Mopsy, and Cotton-tail, his cousin Benjamin, and all his friends. Even the other animals that sometimes tried to eat Peter were invited over. There were **radishes for everyone!**

No one had to worry about being chased by a human, and they were having a **big party** when . . .

Someone new arrived. He was a younger, city version of Mr. McGregor. **Maybe he'd be different**. Maybe he'd be a bit more like Bea.

Or perhaps he'd just leave Peter and his friends alone.

But he was just the same.
Peter and his family had got used
to running wild in the garden.

"This garden is ours,"

Peter said, because rabbits can
speak to one another.

"Nothing has changed."

But **young** Thomas McGregor began to repair
all the walls and fences.

"He doesn't know **anything**," thought Peter.

He could sneak in easily and pull down the flowers.

Next, Thomas McGregor tried an electric fence.

"Hmm," thought Peter.

"More challenging, but perhaps something **we** *can use against* **him**.*"

Peter was a clever rabbit. He got help to send the electricity into the house. Now the only fingers getting fried were Thomas's!

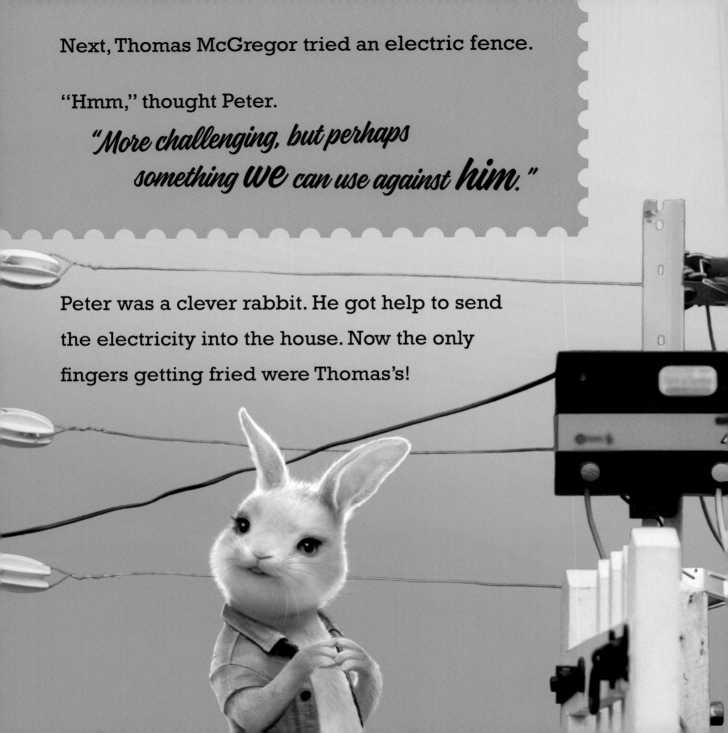

From the garden, Peter could hear young McGregor shout,

"Rab – ZAP – bits!"

"That should do it," Peter said with a smile.

"The garden is ours."

But Thomas McGregor took things a bit too far.
He started throwing explosives around to finish
off Peter **once and for all**.

Pigling Bland, Jemima Puddle-duck, and Mrs. Tiggy-winkle looked on as vegetables **exploded** everywhere.

"I do like my vegetables grilled," Pigling Bland said.

Peter **wasn't** going to let McGregor win. So he let off the last of Thomas's EXPLOSIVES, destroying more of the garden, most of the bunny burrow where Peter and his family lived, and a lot of Bea's house.

Suddenly, Thomas and Peter looked around at the mess.
"Oh no! What have we done?" they both thought.

Peter and Thomas decided to put things right, and made an agreement to **share** the garden.

They still fight. After all, Thomas is **a McGregor** and Peter is **a rabbit**. But for now . . .

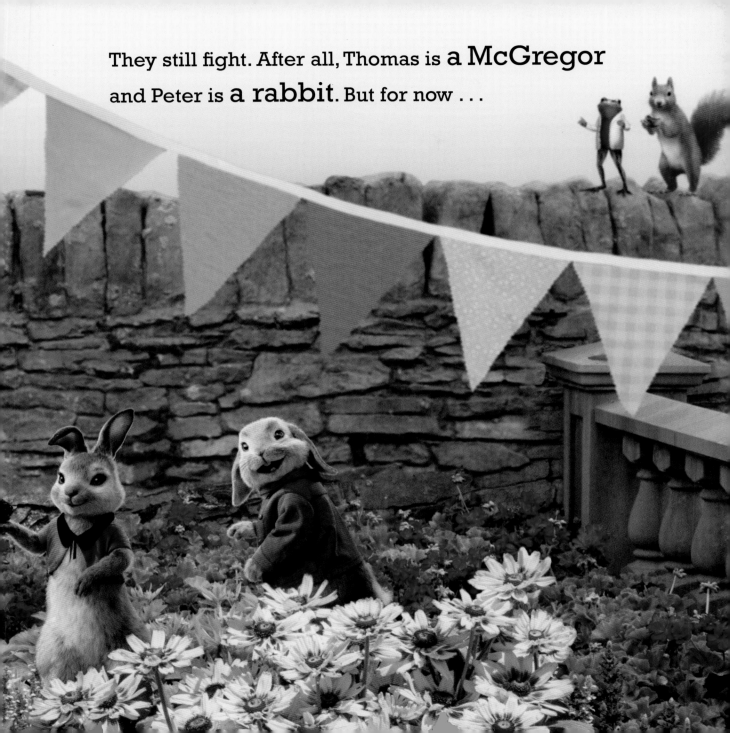

They're giving peace
and **peas** a chance.